Climbing and Diving

Lisa Greathouse

Climbing and Diving

Publishing Credits

Editorial Director
Dona Herweck Rice

Associate Editors
James Anderson
Torrey Maloof

Editor-in-Chief
Sharon Coan, M.S.Ed.

Creative Director
Lee Aucoin

Illustration Manager
Timothy J. Bradley

Publisher
Rachelle Cracchiolo, M.S.Ed.

Science Consultant
Scot Oschman, Ph.D.

Teacher Created Materials
5301 Oceanus Drive
Huntington Beach, CA 92649-1030
http://www.tcmpub.com

ISBN 978-1-4333-0304-3

Printed by: 51497
Printed in: China

Table of Contents

The Science of Diving and Climbing

There are many "extreme sports"—like surfing and snowboarding. But the most extreme sports may be jumping out of airplanes or climbing steep mountains!

Diving and climbing are popular sports all over the world. Many people train hard every year so they can climb the highest mountains. Skydiving is a fast-growing sport. People pay a lot of money to jump from a plane. Watching the Olympics has made diving a "big splash" with a lot of people, too!

But what keeps the climber from falling off the mountain? What slows down the skydiver's parachute? How does the body of a professional diver slice the water with barely a splash? There is a lot of science at work in these sports!

It is a good idea to go climbing with a friend for safety. Besides, someone has to take the pictures!

Diving History

When you think of diving into a pool, you might also think of swimming. But diving really has more in common with gymnastics. Diving became a sport when gymnasts long ago started practicing their sport over water. The sport of diving joined the Olympic Games in 1904.

Greta Johansson, Gold Medal winner, dives in the 1912 Olympics.

Dive Right In!

You climb up the ladder to the diving board and slowly walk to the end of the board. You take a deep breath. It is only a little more than 1 meter (3 feet) off the ground, but it seems like a long way down to the water. You stick your arms up straight over your head. As you bend your knees, your movements make the **springboard** go up and down. With your chin tucked in to your chest, you push off the board with your feet and go headfirst toward the water, following your fingers into the pool.

Diving is fun! You climb out of the pool so you can dive right in again! But diving is more than just a fun sport. There are also many **forces** at work.

Youngest Diver

Thomas Daley of England took up diving at age 8 just because it looked like fun. When he was 10, he won the British championship for divers under 18. At 13, he won the European championship. And at just 14, he became the youngest person to take part in the 2008 Olympics!

Hard Landing

Standing on a platform that is 10 meters (about 33 feet) above the water, Olympic divers plummet at about 64 kilometers (40 miles) per hour. If they hit the water wrong, they can sprain their fingers and toes.

Japan's Mai Nakagawa and Misako Yamashito compete in women's synchronized platform diving in the 2008 Olympics.

Force is indicated by the broken yellow lines. The child pushes up and out with her legs to dive.

Laws of Motion

What happens when you dive off a board? Your body is in **motion**. Motion is how, where, and why something moves. But your body does not move by itself. A force makes it move. A force is a push or a pull that causes movement. When you dive, the force of your leg muscles pushes you off the board—unless someone pushes you from behind!

Isaac Newton

Newton's First Law

There are three laws that tell us about motion. They are based on the work of Isaac Newton. The first law says that an object will keep doing what it is already doing unless a force acts on it. So if something is not moving, it will stay where it is unless a force gets it moving. It also means that a moving object will keep moving in the same direction unless a force makes it stop or change direction.

Newton's Book

Isaac Newton wrote about the laws of motion in his book, the *Principia*. In it, he also explained how the universe works.

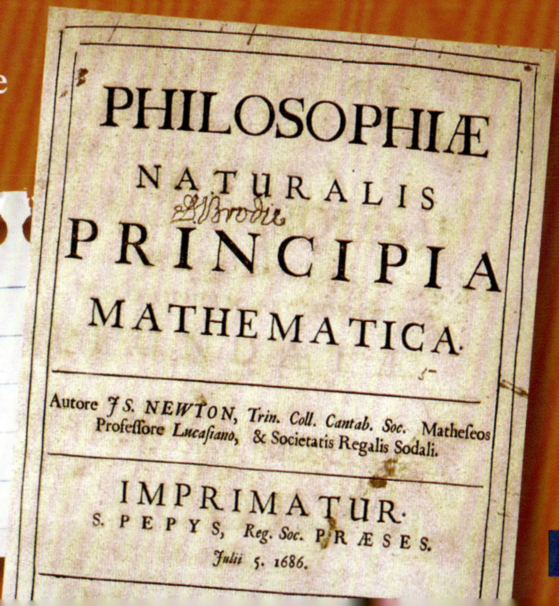

PHILOSOPHIÆ
NATURALIS
PRINCIPIA
MATHEMATICA.

Autore J S. NEWTON, *Trin. Coll. Cantab. Soc.* Matheseos Professore *Lucasiano*, & Societatis Regalis Sodali.

IMPRIMATUR.
S. PEPYS, *Reg. Soc.* PRÆSES.
Julii 5. 1686.

Newton's Second Law

Newton's second law says that when a force acts on an object, the object will speed up or slow down. That is called **acceleration** (ak-sel-uh-RAY-shuhn). The bigger the force, the more the object speeds up or slows down. So, the harder you kick a ball, the faster it bounces across the field. And the more **mass** the object has, the more force you need to move it. That is why it takes more force to throw a bowling ball than a baseball.

Newton's Third Law

The third law says that for every force, there is a reaction. The reaction is equal but opposite to the force. That means that whenever an object pushes another object, it gets pushed back just as hard. When you jump on the edge of a diving board, the board pushes back up on you!

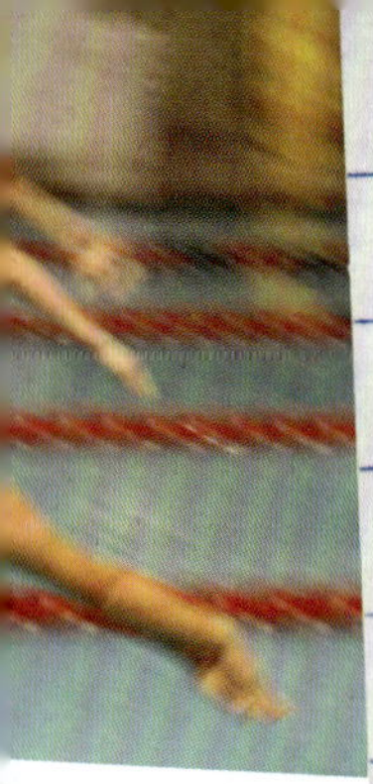

Fall Far, Land Hard

Imagine that you and a friend dive into a pool at the same time from diving boards that are the same height. You will hit the water at the same time—even if your friend is bigger than you. The rate at which you fall will be exactly the same. But if your friend dives off a higher board, he will fall at a faster rate than you. The higher you go, the faster your body accelerates through the air.

Which laws of motion are at work in this activity?

What Goes Up...

Gravity (GRAV-uh-tee) is the main force at work once you jump off a diving board. Gravity is the force that pulls everything toward Earth. It is the force that keeps us on the ground. Gravity pulls a diver downward into the water. Isaac Newton realized that gravity also makes planets go around the sun.

Skydiving

High divers are daring. Skydivers may be even more daring! They jump out of airplanes at 3,000 meters (about 10,000 feet). Gravity is the main force at work when you skydive.

When a skydiver jumps, he or she accelerates fast. The skydiver reaches about 190 kilometers (120 miles) per hour—straight down!—in less than 10 seconds. The diver gains speed with each second. But the faster the diver falls, something slows the diver down. It is air! **Air resistance** is a force. It happens when an object moves through the air. That is because the object must push air out of the way.

Free Fall

Skydivers usually wait about 40 to 60 seconds before opening their parachutes. This is called the "free fall." It gives skydivers the feeling they are flying—and the best views of their lives! When the parachute opens, the relaxing ride to the ground takes 4 to 10 minutes.

Leonardo's Parachute

Skydiving has a long history. Leonardo da Vinci drew some sketches of a parachute more than 500 years ago.

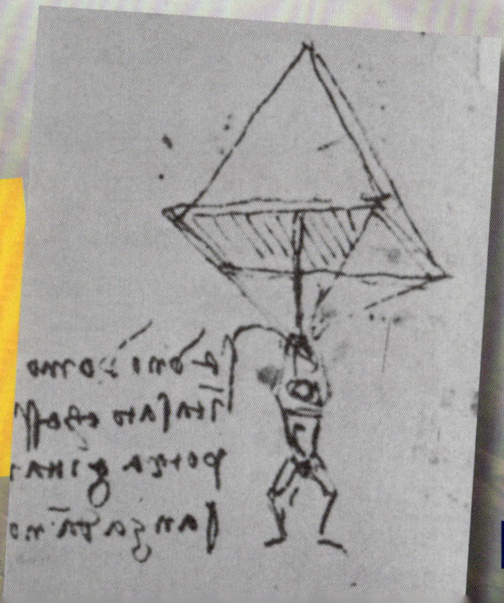

Presidential Skydive

In 1999, former President George H.W. Bush celebrated his 75th birthday with a skydive!

A group of 400 skydivers from 31 nations set a world record in 2006 for the largest connected formation skydive.

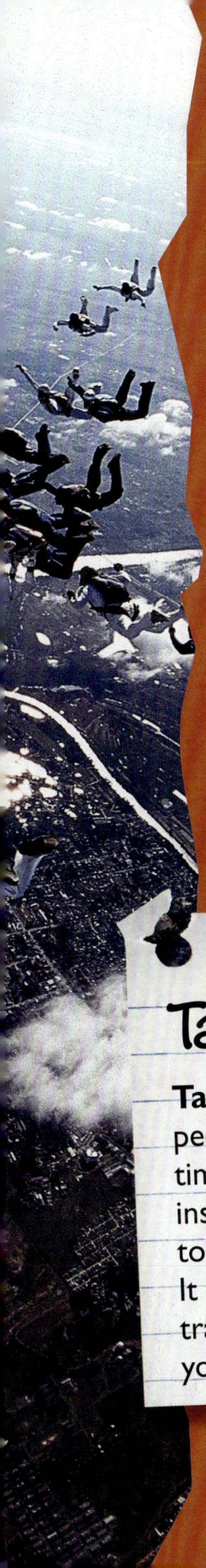

Styles of Falling

There are things that divers can do to slow themselves down or speed themselves up. The skydiver who jumps with arms and legs straight out will drop more slowly than one who falls feet or head first. That is because the person whose arms and legs are straight out has more body parts pushing through the air.

What happens when the skydiver opens the parachute? First, you will see the skydiver go up instead of down. That is because the air resistance is, at first, even stronger than gravity! But finally, gravity wins. The skydiver floats slowly to the ground.

Tandem Diving

Tandem diving is how most people skydive for the first time. You are strapped to an instructor and you jump out together with one parachute. It doesn't require as much training and you still feel like you are flying.

The Perfect Dive

Top divers look like their bodies form straight lines as they dive into pools. That way, they do not run into much air resistance. They do not even make much of a splash. Only their hands enter the water. That makes a tunnel for the rest of the body to follow.

But if you jump off a diving board with your arms and legs straight out to the side, you will not fall nearly as fast. That is because every part of your body is running into air resistance. And you will wind up doing a belly flop into the pool!

Olympic Star

Greg Louganis (loo-GAIN-us) is considered one of the greatest divers of all time. He won his first Olympic medal in 1976 at just 16 years old. In the 1980s, he won four gold medals. He is a six-time world champion and has held 47 national championship titles for the United States.

Speed Suits

What divers wear can slow them down or speed them up. Olympic divers wear special swimsuits that fit like a second skin. They cut down on resistance through the air and in the water. Some skydivers wear something called a wingsuit. It has fabric between the legs and arms, creating a kind of wing. It makes skydivers really feel like they are flying!

Freestyle divers demonstrate their moves.

Dazzling Dives

Jumping out of an airplane or diving off a high board might be enough of a thrill for most people. But others want more. They like to add some dazzle to their dives! Expert divers do tucks, twists, and even backward rolls.

Some skydivers also do stunts before they open their parachutes. This is called freestyle diving. They do spins and tucks, twists and turns. Some even time their tricks with another skydiver!

Diving Dangers

Diving can be dangerous. Thousands of children are injured in diving accidents every year. Always know how deep the water is before you dive. If the water is too **shallow**, you can hit the bottom of the pool and be seriously injured.

Science Friction

Gravity is always working to keep our feet on the ground. So then how are we able to climb mountains? The answer can be found in another force—**friction** (FRIK-shuhn). Friction is a force between two surfaces that rub against each other. Friction slows moving objects. Have you ever poured water on a slide to go faster? The water cuts the friction between you and the slide.

It is the friction between the rock and the climber's hands and feet that keeps the climber from sliding or falling off. Whenever a climber grips a rock, friction helps him or her hold on. Climbers also wear shoes with rubber soles. This gives them extra friction to stick to the rocks.

Cold Climbing

The best seasons for climbing are fall and winter. That is because when rocks are cold, they are easier to hold onto. When rocks are warm, they can become slippery and there is less friction. But some people like to climb on rocks covered in ice and snow. Talk about slippery rocks!

Gravity's Role

Climbing can be a dangerous sport. It takes a lot of training and equipment. So why do people climb rocks or mountains? For one thing, it feels great to reach the top! The view is beautiful. And it is a great way to get close to nature.

But once you reach the top, then what? On the way up, the climber fights gravity. But on the way down, the force of gravity works with the climber. Friction still plays an important part, though. It is what keeps the climber from falling too fast and getting hurt.

This is why many climbers use a harness attached to safety ropes. On the way up, the ropes hold the climber if he or she slips and falls. The rope may be attached to a rock or tree or to another climber. When a cliff or slope is too steep, sometimes climbers **rappel** down. The ropes are attached to a harness and allow the climber to drop down slowly and safely.

Sir Edmund Hillary and Tenzing Norgay

The Biggest Climb

Many climbers dream of climbing Mount Everest. At 8,848 meters (29,029 feet), it is the world's highest mountain. It is on the border between Nepal and Tibet. The first successful climb was in 1953 by Sir Edmund Hillary and Tenzing Norgay. Today, about 2,500 climbers reach the top each year.

Climbing walls are a safe and fun way to practice climbing skills.

Climbing Concerns

Many people climb rocks and mountains to be close to nature. But some people think that the sport is harming nature.

The rule for many climbers is "leave no trace." That means that you leave your path in the same condition as you found it. But climbing can wind up damaging plants and nests. It can also lead to the **erosion** of rocks and soil. Some climbers even leave behind litter.

Some areas have tried to stop climbing. The U.S. National Park Service limits climbing at some popular spots, like Devils Tower National Monument in Wyoming.

Devil's Tower National Monument

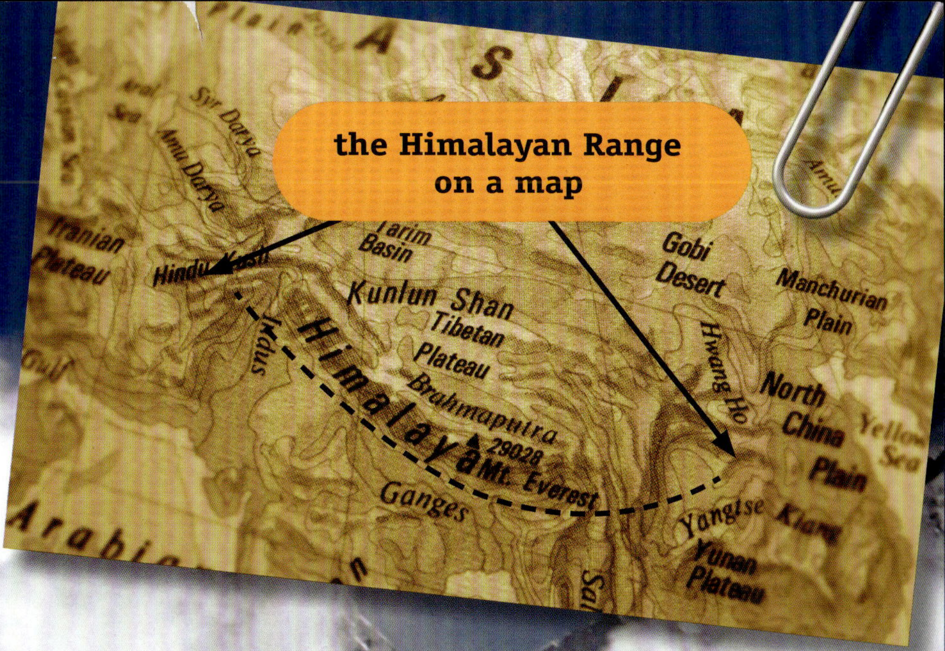

World's 10 Highest Mountains

Rank	Mountain	Range	Country	Meters/Feet
1.	Everest	Himalayas	Nepal / Tibet	8,850 / 29,035
2.	K2 (Mount Godwin Austen)	Karakoram	Pakistan / China	8,611 / 28,250
3.	Kangchenjunja	Himalayas	India / Nepal	8,586 / 28,169
4.	Lhotse	Himalayas	Nepal / Tibet	8,516 / 27,940
5.	Makalu	Himalayas	Nepal / Tibet	8,463 / 27,766
6.	Cho Oyu	Himalayas	Nepal / Tibet	8,201 / 26,906
7.	Dhaulagiri	Himalayas	Nepal	8,167 / 26,795
8.	Manaslu	Himalayas	Nepal	8,163 / 26,781
9.	Nanga Parbat	Himalayas	Pakistan	8,126 / 26,660
10.	Annapurna	Himalayas	Nepal	8,091 / 26,545

How *Extreme* Are You?

Do you want to skydive? Climb a steep mountain? Dive into a pool from a high diving board? Some people love adventures like these. They enjoy the thrills and the dangers. They are willing to take risks for some fun. Other people think the dangers are not worth the risks. Some people are too scared of heights to take the plunge.

Experts say it all depends on your personality. Some people **thrive** on danger. They do best under stress. Others freeze up or panic in life-threatening situations. They prefer to watch.

Which type of person are you?

Fear Factor

There are words for almost every fear you can name. Here are some common ones.

Name	Fear
achluophobia	fear of darkness
acrophobia	fear of heights
agoraphobia	fear of being in public places
algophobia	fear of pain
apiophobia	fear of bees
astraphobia	fear of lightning, thunder
claustrophobia	fear of enclosed spaces
demophobia	fear of crowds
dentophobia	fear of going to the dentist
hematophobia	fear of the sight of blood
ophidiophobia	fear of snakes
triskaidekaphobia	fear of the number 13

Lab: Downhill Racing

Snowboarders wax the bottom of their boards to cut down on friction and help them build up speed. What else would make a snowboard or skateboard change speed?

Materials

- piece of stiff cardboard, at least 45 cm x 30 cm (18 inches x 12 inches)
- blocks or books
- five smooth strips of aluminium foil or waxed paper, each 30 cm x 5 cm (12 inches x 2 inches)
- tape
- small fan
- 120 mL ($\frac{1}{2}$ cup) water
- 15 mL (1 tbsp) butter
- 15 mL (1 tbsp) cornstarch
- salt
- carpenter's square for measuring angle of slope
- checkers
- flag or whistle

Procedure:

1. Tape a short side of each strip of foil or waxed paper to the top edge of the cardboard. Place the strips a minimum of 5 centimeters (2 inches) apart.

2. On the first strip, sprinkle water. On strip two, sprinkle water and salt. On strip three, spread cornstarch. On strip four, spread a thin coat of butter. Position the fan to blow on strip five.

3. Prop the cardboard at a 45-degree angle on books or blocks, creating a slope. Tape the other end of the cardboard to the floor to stabilize it.

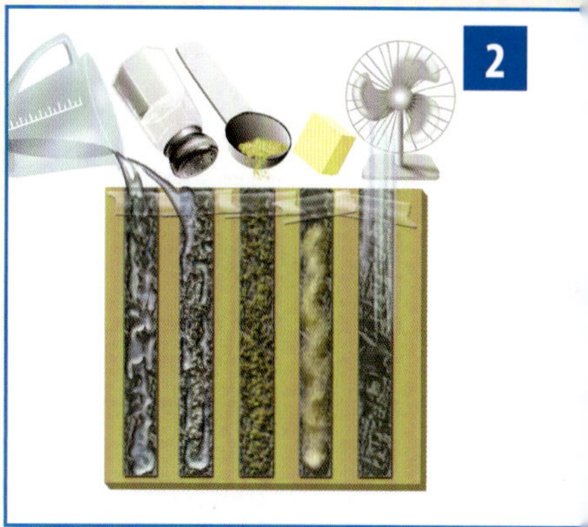

4. Divide the class into five teams. Give each team a checker and assign each team a strip. Wave a flag or blow a whistle to have each team release its checker down its strip at the same time.

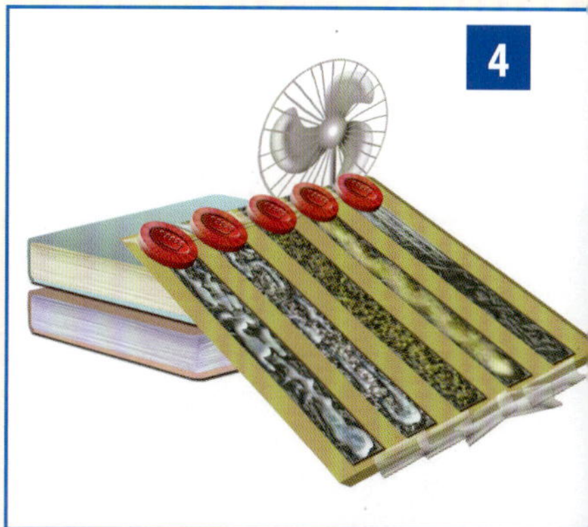

5. Watch to see which checker reaches the bottom first. Record the sequence, first to last, on a chart like the one below.

6. Have students experiment with different slope angles and compare their findings. Does the angle affect the sequence?

Strip sequence	45–degree slope
First place	Strip #_____
Second place	Strip #_____
Third place	Strip #_____
Fourth place	Strip #_____
Fifth place	Strip #_____

Glossary

acceleration—a change in speed

air resistance—force that slows objects that are moving through the air

erosion—wearing away of rocks or soil

force—a push or pull that makes things move

friction—force that acts on surfaces in contact with each other and slows them down

gravity—force that attracts things to each other

mass—amount of matter in an object

motion—a change in position

rappel—to move down an incline with a rope that is let out in segments

shallow—not deep

springboard—diving board with springs

tandem—one following or behind the other

thrive—to flourish or prosper

Index

Scientists Then and Now

Robert Goddard
(1882–1945)

Robert Goddard wanted to explore space. So, he built rockets! Goddard used Newton's laws to help him. He believed that a rocket could travel all the way to the moon. Goddard was the first to launch a liquid-fueled rocket. In 1926, he tested it. It went about 12 meters (40 feet) high at about 97 kilometers (60 miles) per hour. Goddard did not live to see people travel in space, but his ideas and rockets helped pave the way.

Steven Chu
(1948–)

As a child, Steven Chu liked to build things. He started out building model airplanes and ships. Then he saved his lunch money so that he could build rockets at home! In high school, he built a machine that measured gravity. All these childhood experiments would later help him win a Nobel Prize in physics. He also became the Secretary of Energy for President Barack Obama.

Image Credits

Cover PictureArts/Newscom; p.1 PictureArts/Newscom; p.4 2734725246/Shutterstock; p.4-5 Drazen Vukelic/Shutterstock; p.5 Bob Thomas/Popperfoto/Getty Images; p.6 Sportsphoto Ltd./Allstar/Newscom; pp.6-7 Graytown/Dreamstime; p.7 CHINE NOUVELLE/SIPA/Newscom; p.8 Kelly Redinger/Design Pics/Corbis; p.9(top) Christie's Images /SuperStock; p.9(bottom) Jupiterimages Corporation; p.10(top) Larry St. Pierre/Shutterstock; p.10 Fukuoka Irina/Shutterstock; p.10-11 Jupiterimages Corporation; p.12-13 Joggie Botma/Shutterstock; p.13 SPL/Photo Researchers, Inc; p.14 KRT/Newscom; p.14-15 Andi Duff/Alamy; p.15 Atlaspix/Shutterstock; p.16(top) Maryunin Yury Vasilevich/Shutterstock; p.16(bottom) AFP/Getty Images; p.16-17 PictureArts/Newscom; p.18 PictureArts/Newscom; p.18-19 PictureArts/Newscom; p.19 phdpsx/Shutterstock; p.20-21 Greg Epperson/Shutterstock; p.21 Cyril Hou/Shutterstock; p.22-23(bottom) jon challicom/Alamy; p.22-23 Danny Warren/Shutterstock; p.23 t14/ZUMA Press/Newscom; p.24 Mike Norton/Shutterstock; p.24-25 Jupiterimages Corporation; p.25 Sean Gladwell/Shutterstock; p.26-27 Drazen Vukelic/Shutterstock; p.29(top) Ben Heys/Shutterstock; p.29 Nicolle Rager Fuller; p.32 (left) Nasa; p.32 (right) Roy Kaltschmidt/Lawrence Berkeley National Labratory